ADRIAN TOWNSEND

TEACHERS' TALES

Illustrated by Matthew Bunce

To Brandon

Best wishes

Adrian Townsend

First Published 2004
By
Grassy Hill Publishing
52 Wheatley Road Garsington Oxford
OX44 9ER

ISBN 1-903569-07-9

To

Mike and Jackie Friend

Contents

Technical Tandy

Mr J W Tandy is the head teacher of Pikedown Primary School. You can read this on the notice board outside the school gates. You're supposed to be able to read this on the school's Internet website but if you type in the web address, you get a picture of a villa in Tuscany mixed with information about Fender Stratocaster guitars. Mr Tandy goes to Italy every summer for his holidays and he loves guitars. He plays his guitar in assembly. He plugs a computer into a large TV screen and the words come up on the screen as he plays his guitar. He makes everybody sing along. Nobody minds the singing. Mr Tandy is a good musician and the songs are great. The trouble with Mr Tandy is that he likes gadgets.

Pikedown School is full of gadgets.

There are gadgets in the staff room, gadgets in every classroom, gadgets in the corridors and, of course, gadgets in his office. At the last count, Mr Tandy's office contained; one surveillance monitor, two desktop computers, a shredder, a voice-activated hands-free telephone, two electronic organisers, a solar powered pencil sharpener, loudspeakers that look like picture frames, a clockwork radio, a laser-controlled pointing device, a scanner, a DVD player, a digital camera, a bracelet blood pressure monitor and an 'ergonomically designed' cappuccino coffee maker from Milan.

The last count of the gadgets in Mr Tandy's office was on Friday 22nd May. Zak Goldman does an unofficial Year 6 event every term. He counts what he can see when he goes into Mr Tandy's office, nothing covered with papers and nothing in his cupboard.

Zak reckoned Mr Tandy had increased his

total gadget collection by 12% in the last 6 months.

"Mind you, I haven't seen the motorised football inflator for a while. We may have to remove that from the official list," said Zak. Zak's dad is an accountant and also Chair of Governors. He calls Mr Tandy, Joe.

We all call him Jammy Tandy. He got the nickname because of his gadgets and because he's lucky. He thinks his gadgets are wonderful. He thinks gadgets are great. The trouble is, none of Mr Tandy's gadgets work properly. Everybody knows this. Everybody except Mr Tandy. He's always telling us how wonderful technology is. No one wants to upset him so no one tells him the truth. Last year we thought he'd got the message when some things went a bit wrong in school. Mostly his gadgets were to blame but as usual he got lucky: Jammy Tandy. Here's what happened.

It all began with Mrs Hedges, the school cook. She's friends with Mr Thompson, the school caretaker. Together, they know a lot about the school and Mr Tandy's gadgets. Anyway, Mrs Hedges was in school early as usual, getting ready to cook the school dinners. She fumbled in her bag for her keys to the kitchen, only to remember what Mr Thompson had said the night before.

"Remember you won't need your keys in the morning. Mr Tandy's new security system will be fitted by then. All the doors will have new electronic number pad locks. You just have to tap in your own security number for your own door. Yours is 79546."

Mr Thompson made Mrs Hedges say the number three times so she wouldn't forget. But she did forget, and now she couldn't get into the school kitchen. It took her twenty minutes to track down Mr Thompson and by the time he let her in, she was running late to get the fish fingers ready.

"I can't be doing with these numbers," she said to Mr Thompson. "Can't you do something with the keypad and leave me with the old lock and key?"

Mr Thompson is a dab hand with most things, but not electrics. Still, he likes a challenge, so he said he'd see what he could do. In truth, he wasn't pleased to have numbers to remember either. He liked his keys. He had a nice, clanking, tinkling set of keys. He hung them from the belt on his trousers. He is an opener of doors not a number cruncher. Mr Thompson decided to experiment with his new number pad. After three lost screws and a couple of mild electric shocks, Mr Thompson found the answer; a thin piece of card 1cm wide by 3cm long. By trial and error, Mr Thompson had discovered that you could stop the number keypad from working, by jamming the thin piece of card in a small slit at the back of the keypad. It helped if you loosened a couple of special screws on the front and Mrs Hedges had a tool for this. Once the card was inside the pad, all you had to do was move it about until the pad bleeped and hey presto, you didn't need the key pad anymore. Mr Thompson fixed his own lock, then the one on the kitchen door for Mrs Hedges. She told Mrs Patterson the school secretary, and she had her lock 'fixed' as well. They all continued to use their old-fashioned keys. The building was still secure, but Mrs Hedges, Mrs Patterson and Mr Thompson just didn't need 'New Technology'.

The thin pieces of card worked well for several weeks. Jammy Tandy didn't know about them and he was as proud as punch with his new security system. "No need for all those keys now," he said to Mr Thompson every time he saw him with his bunch of keys. "We're a technically advanced school, free from the chains of the past." Mr Tandy smiled at the phrase he had just used and he used it again in assembly later on in the morning. Assembly is a good time to see Mr Tandy in action with his gadgets. There was no guitar today. Instead it was poetry assembly and Mr Tandy was using his latest hands-free microphone that he'd bought for the school. Jody Richardson from Class 2 was about to read her wonderful poem about worms to everyone. Jody stepped forward and Mr Tandy placed the small microphone on a kind of necklace around Jody's neck. "The helping hand of technology for small voices," he said. "Off you go, Jody."

At the back of the hall, we could see Jody's mouth moving but we heard nothing. Mr Tandy dashed to the amplifier and turned a few knobs. We heard a loud whistling noise, then a crackle, then a whizzing noise and finally Jody's voice halfway through her poem.

"Hold on, Jody. Stop, Jody. I don't think everyone heard the beginning," he said. "Start again, Jody." Jody started her poem again. This is how it went.

Worms are wriggly – *whistle* (Mr Tandy turns a knob)
Worms are – *screech* (Mr Tandy turns another knob)
Worms are (silence) worms are gr... – *screech* (Mr Tandy frowns)
Worms are s... and (silence) ...ubbly
(Mr Tandy turns another knob)
Worms are MY best (silence)
Things to EAT.

After her poem, Jody looked up and smiled. Mr Tandy smiled but looked red in the face and everyone else burst into applause. Lisa Faraway said it was a relief to clap

because she'd been biting her fingers hard
to stop herself from laughing.

Anyway, Mr Tandy thanked Jody and told
everyone to sit up straight, ready to go out of
the hall. He pointed the remote control at
the stereo, ready to start Beethoven's Piano
Concerto for the music to go out from

assembly. The hall lights went out and a loud blast of a radio phone-in filled the hall. Nobody said anything. We'd seen it all before. Mr Tandy went red again and rushed to the on-off switch

After assembly it was playtime. Mr Tandy went to the staffroom for coffee. Three teachers were standing outside, fiddling with the keypad. Mr Tandy helped them get in. Once inside, Mr Tandy clapped his hands.

"Excuse me, everyone" he announced. "Can I just remind you to make use of the new electronic, touch sensitive staff notice board" and he pointed to a large white notice board at the far end of the staffroom. "It's there to save you time and work. We can all communicate electronically now. All you have to do is press one of the touch-screen menus. They will open sub menus to help you communicate, or you can use the electronic pen to write directly on to the screen if you wish. It's just like a giant electronic organiser. There are sections for appointments, meetings, curriculum details and professional announcements. There's even an 'inspirational thoughts for the day' section. Look! I'll enter a couple of those to get us started, then you can all give it a try – just play with it for a couple of days, then we'll have a proper training session at next week's staff meeting. Don't worry if you go wrong, just press clear and it will wipe itself clean". Mr Tandy turned to the notice board and entered three thoughts for the day.

No.1 Aim for your target but focus on the child.

No.2 Good teachers are organised – great teachers have clear objectives.

No.3 The path to an effective classroom starts with differentiated planning.

Mr Tandy was pleased to see the new messages shining into the staffroom. He turned to gauge his teachers' reactions but most of them had left. Only Mrs Phelps was waiting and she handed Mr Tandy a note about geography books. Mr Tandy made his way back to his office. He was a bit disappointed that no-one seemed to like the new notice board and he punched his personal security number into the new keypad. Back in his office, he got on with some very important statistical analysis.

Halfway through a mathematical equation that would prove the school test scores were the best in the country, the sky outside went very dark. Rain poured down, bouncing off the hard surfaces in the school, making a noise like gunfire. This was followed by an almighty flash of lightning. The lights went out. Mr Tandy's computer and all the other gadgets in his office went dark and silent. Mr Tandy saw sparks shoot from his wonderful new door lock.

The lightning strikes had caused a power cut. Mr Tandy looked at his silent gadgets and frowned.

Thunder and lightning make children excitable. Mr Tandy knew he had to make a quick tour of the classrooms to check everything was ok. He went to the door but couldn't get out. He typed his security number into the lock but still the door didn't open. He tried again – still nothing. A small feeling of panic crept into Mr Tandy's brain. Regaining control of himself, he reached for the telephone. There was no dialling tone, so he called Mrs Patterson on the internal line. "I seem to be stuck in my office, Jean," he said, "can you come and tap in my number from the outside keypad?" Mr Tandy put the phone down and waited and waited. He was just about to telephone Mrs Patterson again when he heard her voice outside his office door.

"It's no good, Mr Tandy, I've tried it six or seven times but it doesn't want to open. The keypad isn't working. It seems to be broken. Shall I go and get Mr Thompson?"

"No, no, hang on a minute," Mr Tandy shouted back through the door, "these locks are hi-tech equipment. Mr Thompson may not know what to do."

Mr Tandy did not want a school caretaker rough handling his hi-tech equipment. He knew what Mr Thompson thought of the keypads. It would be too much to put up with. Mr Thompson would gloat for days. He'd never let him forget about it. "Chains of the past – chains of the future" is probably what he'd say.

"No, no, I've a better idea," said Mr Tandy. "Look Jean, this stuff is high grade electronic equipment. Let's just let it settle in for a bit. I'm sure when this thunderstorm passes over, it will settle down. It's probably electro-static build up. I'll just get on with my work in here for a while. I've got plenty to do. I'll try it later. If it doesn't fix itself by the end of the day, we can call the company who fitted it – when the children have gone home. Oh, and, er, Jean, no one else needs to know about this. Stick a notice on my door. Keep people away. Tell anyone who calls I'm in an important meeting. I think that's best. Don't you?"

Mrs Patterson didn't know what to say. She couldn't help smiling at the thought of Mr Tandy stuck in his office with nowhere to go. She still thought it best to get Mr Thompson with his toolkit but she was a good school secretary; she knew when she shouldn't laugh.

"Well, if you're sure, Mr Tandy," she said with raised eyebrows. "I'll just write out the note for the door and pin it up."

So that was how Mr Tandy got stuck inside his office with a note saying 'Important meeting – do not disturb' on the outside of his door.

Only Jamie Purbrick from class 2B came to see Mr Tandy, but Mrs Patterson told him that he would have to come back later. Mr Tandy was busy.

Mr Tandy <u>was</u> busy, he had lots of paperwork to do, and for a while he quite liked the idea that he <u>had</u> to get on with it. He just couldn't get away from it. By lunchtime he had filled in several forms and written six letters, but now he was getting hungry. He looked at his watch. "Good grief," he said, "lunchtime already," and he got up to go to the hall for dinner. He stopped halfway to the door. "Silly me," he said, and realising he needed food, he telephoned Mrs Patterson.

"Can you get Mrs Hedges to send me a dinner over to my office please, Jean?" Tell her to send it to the window. I'll take it through the window." Mr Tandy had thought

21

about climbing out of the window but he knew it wouldn't look dignified, and anyway, the windows had been adjusted so they could only open halfway, to keep burglars out. Now they kept him in.

"What a carry on," he thought to himself. "Stuck in my own office. I'll be a laughing stock if this gets out." He was still thinking how unfair life could be when there was a tap at the window. It was Mrs Hedges with the tray of dinner.

"I've been told to bring it to your window, Mr Tandy," said Mrs Hedges, "I've been told not to come into your office. I know I'm only the school cook so you don't have to let me into your office, you don't have to tell me about your important meetings, but passing dinner through windows doesn't seem right, Mr Tandy. Certainly not. You're a headmaster, Mr Tandy, you should know that. Oh well, who am I to say? I'm only the cook. I only cook food, I don't know about meetings. Nobody tells me nothing. Here you are then. You've got two lots of potatoes. Mind you don't spill the gravy."

Mrs Hedges squeezed the plate through the half open window. "Enjoy your dinner, Mr Tandy. I expect when you've finished your meeting, you'll let me know about the washing up."

"Oh yes, thank you very much, Mrs Hedges. You're too kind. You're a wonderful cook and very helpful."

"Hmph," said Mrs Hedges, and she strode back to her kitchen.

It wasn't the window or the dinner that bothered Mrs Hedges, it was the not knowing. Why hadn't she been told about an important meeting? Mr Tandy hadn't told her, Mr Thompson hadn't told her and Jean Patterson had only told her at the last minute. Then she was expected to take

23

dinners to windows. No, this wasn't good enough. Mrs Hedges had to get to the bottom of this. So, when dinner had been served and cleared away, she stormed into Jean Patterson's office.

"Look Jean, I don't ask much, I only need to know...time and time again...school cooks left out..." Mrs Patterson had heard it all before, but she nodded and said "yes" and "no" in the right places, until Mrs Hedges had finished. It was only then that she smiled.

"I don't think it's funny, Jean," said Mrs Hedges.

"But it is, Wendy," said Mrs Patterson. "It is funny. It's not you, it's Mr Tandy. You see, Wendy, he couldn't come for his dinner. He's stuck in his office." She looked around to see if anyone else was listening, then she whispered it again. "Mr Tandy's stuck in his office. It's that blooming electronic keypad lock thing – it's blown up. He's stuck in there.

25

But you're not supposed to know. Keep it under your hat. He said I couldn't tell anyone – but I can trust you. You're the school cook."

Mrs Patterson and Mrs Hedges looked at each other and burst out laughing. "Well, I've heard of two old ladies stuck in the lavatory, but never one headmaster stuck in his office," said Mrs Hedges and they laughed again.

"What's so funny, girls?" came a voice from the door. It was Mrs Hewton, the deputy head. She doesn't like being left out of things either and she too was let in on the secret. Somehow Mr Thompson found out as well and soon all the teachers and dinner ladies knew about Mr Tandy, stuck in his office.

It cheered up the staffroom no end.

"I expect he's playing with his scanner in there," said Mrs Jones, laughing.

"Or monitoring his heartbeat after a stressful morning of paperwork," said Mrs Phelps.

"Perhaps he's making cappuccino for

Senorita Silviatore, his secret Italian girlfriend," said Mrs Gould, and everyone in the staffroom fell about laughing.

"We could have a new school song," said Miss Ross. "We could call it 'Tandy's old Gadgetry" and she started singing.

> "Oh dear, what can the matter be?
> Mr Tandy's stuck with his gadgetry,
> Oh dear, what can the matter be?
> Nobody knows he is there!"

By this time, the singing and laughing was so loud, it could be heard outside the staffroom door. Mr Tandy could hear the happy, laughing voices in his office. He picked up the internal telephone and rang the staff room. Mrs Hewton answered,

"Yes, Mr Tandy, no, Mr Tandy, fine, Mr Tandy, I understand, Mr Tandy." and she put the phone down.

"Well, girls, Mr Tandy asked if we are all ok, he heard laughing. He says he's busy, not to be disturbed, but if you've got any important messages for him, to put them on the electronic notice board."

"Oh, I've got one," said Mrs Gould, and she picked up the new electronic pen and wrote on the notice board:

' Dear Mr Tandy, when you are stuck in your office, remember to adjust your batteries.' Everybody laughed.

"Give me that thing," said Miss Ross, and she wrote on the board:

'Good teachers are everywhere -great teachers are underpaid'. Everyone cheered.

"My turn," said Mrs Phelps, and she wrote:

'The path to an inspirational weekend starts with two glasses of wine'. "Here, here, and "Quite right," all the teachers shouted, and soon everyone had their first ever goes on the electronic notice board. It was full of

messages for Mr Tandy. One even said,

"Remember, you promised to take Jason Pickering out of my class FOREVER."

As well as laughing, all the teachers agreed the newfangled notice board was 'not bad'. They only stopped using it when the bell went for the end of dinnertime.

"Right, ladies," said Mrs Hewton. "Playtime over. Back to the grind. You'd better clear that notice board before he sees it." Mrs Phelps pressed the 'clear' button but nothing happened, all the messages were still there.

"Try it again," urged Mrs Hewton. Buttons were pressed, bleeps were heard, but still all the messages remained on the screen.

"Oh, Crikey! What will he say if he sees this lot?" said Mrs Hewitt. "Jean, put a cloth over it. I'll try and clear it later."

Afternoon registration in Pikedown School was called by happy, smiling, slightly worried-looking teachers.

Back in his office, as the afternoon wore on, Mr Tandy was getting anxious. He didn't want to be locked in at the end of the day. "If the worst comes to the worst," he said to himself, "I'll have to let Thompson break the door down. I'll never hear the end of it but at least I'll be able to get home." Mr Tandy decided to get on with some more paperwork. He finished writing some overhead projector notes for an important parents' meeting that was going to take place in the school on Thursday.

Mr Tandy was pleased that he'd got so much done. He decided to practise a bit of the talk he was going to deliver to the parents. He picked up his battery-operated laser pointer and put the first overhead on the projector.

"Targets are important for a school," began Mr Tandy. "Clear, focused, manageable targets," he continued, and he pointed his laser to the words 'clear', 'focused' and 'manageable' as he spoke.

"I'm glad I bought this gadget," said Mr Tandy as he examined his lovely laser pointer in his hand. He turned the light on and off. He began to play with it. He became Darth Vader with a light sabre. He zapped the beam on and off around the room. He flashed the light at a letter from a parent. "You are not clear." Zap! He flashed the light pointer at a plan of the National Curriculum. "You are not manageable." Zap! "And you..." He looked around his room for something else to zap. "You," he said, his eyes peering at the electronic lock on his door, "you are not focused." Zap! And he flashed the light onto the keypad lock. As he did, all the lights in the school came on again. Mr Tandy's CD player came to life, Beethoven's Piano Concerto filled his office. A spurt of steam came from his cappuccino machine. His digital answer phone told him he wasn't available and wonder of wonders, best of all, smoke came from his electronic keypad and his office door sprung open.

Mr Tandy stood, light sabre in hand, master of his universe.

The flashing lights told Mrs Hewton that something had happened. She knew she had to check out the staff notice board. She told her class to get on quietly and rushed to the staffroom. On the way, she saw Mr Tandy's open door. She caught sight of him just going into the staffroom.

"Mr Tandy," she called, "are you alright? I saw your door open and some smoke? Have you finished your meeting?"

"Yes, I'm fine, thank you Mrs Hewton. The storm caused a few problems but I've got a lot done in my office. I'm just going to see if the staff have left me any messages on the new notice board." Mr Tandy strode into

32

the staff room. Mrs Hewton ran after him.

"Oh, there's a cloth over the board,' said Mr Tandy. "Is something wrong?"

Mrs Hewton pushed past Mr Tandy and ran to the electronic board.

"No, no, not at all," said Mrs Hewton. "It's just, you know, all these electrical problems today. The teachers thought it would be best covered up in the storm to keep it safe until it's checked out."

"I suppose they're right," said Mr Tandy. "I'm going to get the electricians in. I think the new electronic key locks may be overdoing the school's old electrical system. I think I'll get them taken out." Mrs Hewton smiled and nodded as she glanced nervously at the staff notice board. "Do you know, Pat," Mr Tandy continued. "Sometimes I think the staff just humour me about my technological advances. Tell me honestly, Pat, do the teachers really like that new notice board?

They don't seem to use it much."

"Well," said Mrs Hewton. "I'm sure they'll get used to it. They just need to see how useful it is. They just need to... enjoy it a bit" and she lifted a corner of the cloth over the screen, "I think, I think its ok." She smiled as she looked further under the cloth. "After all, Mr Tandy, technology is the future. As you say, it's time saving, it's focused and," Mrs Hewton pulled the cloth away from the screen.
"It's CLEAN!"

Clicking Carter

Suzy Winthorpe didn't really want to work the early shift today, but she knew it was her turn. Her best friend, Jenny Tyler had stayed at her Nan's last night, so she couldn't get to school early. Suzy, didn't like getting to school before she had to, but she did her duty and arrived outside the school gates at 8.15, just in time to begin the Tuesday operations of Carter-watch.

Suzy and Jenny started Carter-watch in January and it was now well into the summer only another four weeks to go before they both left Parkhill Primary FOR GOOD. In September, they would be at secondary school surrounded by cool people at last. No more little kids and no more Ms Carter. Jenny and Suzy had both really liked being at Parkhill Primary School.

They specially liked the school plays they'd been in and the trips to activity centres but all of that, all of the good things had taken place in the time before Carter. Carter had arrived and ruined everything. How could the arrival of a new headteacher spoil their lives completely? Mrs Williams, their old headteacher was brilliant. She laughed a lot, let girls play football, made jokes and most important of all dressed sensibly.

Mrs Williams dressed like a proper teacher. She wore sensible skirts and jumpers only a touch of make up, and her colours were teacher like; plain and dull. Mrs Williams played by the rules. Jenny and Suzy didn't need to do a Williams-watch, Mrs. Williams clothes were pretty much the same everyday, but last January, from the moment the girls clocked Ms Carter they knew they had to keep a special eye on what she was wearing.

The plan began quite informally; Suzy and Jenny found themselves talking about Ms Carter's appearance each playtime. It was when Ms Carter introduced a new school uniform and new school rules that Suzy and Jenny decided to get serious. They decided upon revenge. They hatched their simple plan to keep a diary of all the outfits that Ms Carter wears everyday, make notes of changes, colour clashes, wrong-make up, bad hair and then – and this is the best – then write an article for their favourite teenage magazine called *'Go Girl'*. Their article would be called *'No Style – the diary of an uncool headteacher, how to get it all wrong.'*

Suzy and Jenny had got pages and pages of diary notes. It was hard work writing it all down, that was why it was important to have an early shift for Carter watch. By getting to school early, they could write down most of her details before school started. That left lunchtime and after school to note down the day's other changes.

Suzy fumbled in her bag to check that she'd got the Carter-watch diary with her. Safe and sound inside an old plastic lunch box. Teachers have a way of snooping inside school bags. As long as the diary was well hidden no one else would know. Just as Suzy closed her bag, Ms Carter swung into view; the first sighting of the day. The school gates were already open so Ms Carter swung her silver grey, open top Mercedes sports car carefully into the car park. Suzy took in what she could. An open top day, so Ms Carter was wearing sunglasses. Suzy knew they were *Korocho Kavano* because she'd seen them before. She didn't need to check the gold KK's on the side. With the sunglasses she was wearing a sun hat. Oh dear! A *Rancho* baseball cap with a tie-up back and yes, horror of horrors, Ms Carter had used the ties to keep her hair in place.

Suzy hurried into the playground. Ms Carter was waiting for the car roof to fold itself down like a large butterfly. This gave Suzy a chance to check what was playing on the sound system. Uh! Suzy recognised it as something her dad played a lot, U2, and loud! Ms Carter zapped the car shut, picked up her red leather *Manraos* briefcase and gave Suzy her first opportunity to check the entire outfit. Today was a suit day; a powder blue miniskirt with matching jacket, lemon chiffon blouse and, oh good grief! pale purple Aztec shoes with sling backs and high heels. How does she drive in those?

"Good morning, Ms Carter," said Suzy. "Good morning" (pause) "Suzy," said Ms Carter as she stood still and looked closely at Suzy.

Suzy could feel Ms Carter's steely eyes examining her. She felt herself go red as Ms

Carter checked her up and down.

"Socks, Suzy, Socks, get them straight and keep your skirt with the buckle at the front. Remember you represent Parkhill School in everything you do. Standards, Suzy, high standards. You are what the world sees. You're at a good school now." Ms Carter turned and strode into her office.

Suzy fiddled with the buckle on the front of her skirt. Her skirt. It was skirts that started everything. When Ms Carter first arrived at the school most people gave her a chance. They put up with the new school rules: the 'Golden Silence' in assembly, the extra homework, even the 'football is not for girls' pronouncement. No, it was the skirt or rather new skirt that did it. Ms Carter announced that she was introducing a brand new school uniform: a uniform that would raise the profile of the school, a uniform that would stand for traditional academic excellence. For Suzy and Jenny that turned out to be the *skirt* or rather the *kilt*. The new school colours were yellow, and wait for it, chocolate brown. Everyone had to wear a brown blazer with bright yellow edging all the way around. With the blazer went a tie, a stripy yellow and brown tie, and the skirts for girls (no trousers) were tartan yellow and brown with additional *pale* blue added. They were, they **are** hideous. Made from heavy wool they are very scratchy, especially in the summer.

Suzy straightened her socks and scratched her knees where her skirt rubbed. "Yes, Ms Carter, you'll pay for this" thought Suzy to herself. At first, quite a few parents objected to the new uniform. Some said it was a waste of money and lots of people reminded Ms Carter that Parkhill School is not in Scotland. "The design is English tartan" Ms Carter informed them. "When the new uniform becomes known around the town, you will be proud your children are wearing it," she said. Anyway, that seems to be what happened. People in the town remarked about the school with the posh uniform. Jenny's dad said he changed his mind after the parents meeting with Ms Carter. He told Jenny that Ms Carter seemed "well turned out herself" and "we should give her a chance." It was when Suzy and Jenny realised that they had no hope, they hatched the Carterwatch plan. Suzy hurried into her classroom. Quickly she noted down her observations in the Carter watch diary. Because she had to straighten her skirt and socks, she hadn't had time to check the Carter accessories, jewellery, make-up etc. Still, she and Jenny could do it together in assembly. In fact, assembly was the best time of all for Carter-watch. Assembly provided twenty minutes of full blown Ms Carter on her own, no distractions just pure undiluted Carter.

It's a good job that school assembly is just before morning play. It means that Jenny and Suzy don't have to remember all the Carter watch observations for too long before they can write them down in the playground. When Jenny arrived at school, Suzy filled her in on the first sightings of the day and they were both now ready to pay careful attention in assembly.

Jenny and Suzy are in Yale class in Parkhill school and just before assembly, Miss Jones their class teacher reminded them again about the rules for assembly; walk in without touching each other, sit still, look forward, listen, no coughing and above all, silence at all times. Silence brings reflection; reflection is the shiny gold of thought – Golden Silence. As Suzy, Jenny and Yale class walked without touching along the corridor to the assembly hall, Jenny wondered why if silence is so golden it had to be filled every assembly time with Vivaldi. The music of the week; Vivaldi's *Four Seasons*. Jenny wondered if she might actually prefer silence.

Yale class made their way into the hall. Stanford, Harvard, Princeton, Cornell and Columbia classes were already there. Yale waited at the door before silently walking their line across the hall to take their place.

Ms Carter was at the front doing her prowl. As each class entered the hall she looked long and hard at them. Then she followed them with her eyes as they sat down boy, girl, boy, girl on the floor. Next she walked up and down in front of the lines of children as they sat silently looking forward. She spotted Matt Smith glancing round at Sophie. CLICK. Ms Carter clicked her fingers. Her outstretched arm and pointed finger identified the rule breaker, one Golden Silence point lost to Stanford. Up and down, Ms Carter prowled;

CLICK an outstretched arm at Mark Ball for shuffling. Up and down CLICK the arm stretched out to Katie Gordon for coughing. CLICK to Rebecca Goodron for not looking forward. Ms Carter was clicking well today. The prowling time was good for Carter-watch. Jenny and Suzy noticed that Ms Carter had chosen gold for her earrings and necklace. Gold long drop, pear shaped earrings and a small gold choker necklace. They both glistened in the morning sun. "No, not gold with pale blue," thought Jenny. "The proportions are all wrong. The earrings are too large, the necklace too small." Jenny made a mental note. Ms Carter continued to prowl. CLICK an outstretched arm found Jason Campbell. It also displayed a brightly coloured bracelet on Ms Carter's wrist. Jenny and Suzy both stared open mouthed as they caught sight of it. It was multicoloured and made of precious stones, opals, diamonds, rubies and others. As it dangled on the end of Ms Carter's wrist, it made a soft jingling sound as Ms Carter moved her arm. It reflected the light in the hall. It threw shadows of multicoloured light. It was expensive, it was classy and it was very BEAUTIFUL. Jenny and Suzy didn't risk looking at each other but they both knew what they were thinking. WOW! This was not Carter. This was something else. In all their weeks of Carter-watch they'd never seen one piece with so much style. WOW! Carter with a piece of STYLE. "Still, it doesn't go with the earrings" thought Jenny.

Once everyone was in the hall, Ms Carter got on with her assembly. Striving, standards, being the best – it was a theme that Suzy and Jenny had heard before. Suzy distracted herself by taking mental notes about Ms Carter's nail polish. Jenny was concentrating on make up – too much eye shadow and cheap blusher. They were both longing for the bell for playtime when Ms Carter began one of her prowls along the line of children as she was talking. Suddenly she noticed Josh Atkins cleaning his glasses on his tie.

"You, you boy, stop that," shouted Ms Carter and she shot her arm at Josh and clicked her fingers. Josh, who was sitting between Jenny and Suzy, looked straight up at Ms Carter's finger. He looked startled. Flashes of coloured reflected light from Ms Carter's bracelet sped towards him. The jingle of Ms Carter's bracelet played a haunting tune like Tibetan wind chimes. Jenny and Suzy both felt an amazing power shoot between them. They felt their hair sucked towards it. They felt drawn towards it and even at the risk of loosing a Golden Silence point, they turned to look at Josh. He wasn't there, he had disappeared. Suzy and Jenny both hurriedly looked back to Ms Carter. She was standing with her arm outstretched, still pointing to the gap on the floor where Josh wasn't. Her mouth was open, her nostrils were wide and a look of astonishment was frozen onto her face.

She regained control, lowered her arm and as calmly as she could, she looked around the room. Everyone was waiting for her to continue her talk about standards. No-one else was shocked. The hall was full of the usual

semi-bored assembly expressions. No-one else had noticed that Josh Atkins had disappeared. Only Suzy, Jenny and Ms Carter knew and Ms Carter knew that Jenny and Suzy knew.

Ms Carter gathered herself, finished her assembly and sent everyone out to play. Jenny and Suzy ran to their favourite place behind the old concrete steps that lead into the boiler room.

"Crikey! What about that?" shouted Jenny.

"I knew you saw it," said Suzy.

"Those flashing lights, the mysterious sounds and the next thing he's gone. I've never seen anything like it," said Jenny.

"Oh my god, Josh has gone. She's made him disappear. She's blooming well zapped him."

"What has she done?"

"What are we going to do?"
Suzy and Jenny didn't have to wait long to find out. After play, just as they were beginning Maths, they were called to Ms Carter's office. Suzy straightened her skirt before knocking on the door.

"Come in," called Ms Carter. Suzy and Jenny edged nervously into Ms Carter's office. "Socks, Jenny, socks, one up, one down! Show some decorum young lady."

Jenny tidied her socks and for what seemed a very long time, Jenny and Suzy stood staring at Ms Carter as she stood silently staring back at them. Eventually she began.

"Girls, I've asked you to come and see me because I think you may be able to help me, er...the school, that is, with a matter of school improvement. As you know I've only been here since last January and I have still got to get to know everyone. I am gradually building up my knowledge of all the pupils in the school by talking to them...and their friends and I'd like to talk to you about a friend in your class, Joshua Atkins. I must say, already I think he's an individual, especially the way he uses his tie." Ms Carter laughed nervously. Jenny and Suzy smiled without commitment. "Anyway, Joshua. Can you tell me a bit about him? What sort of things does he like to do? Err, do you know his parents? What are they like, what do they do?"

"My mum and dad know them quite well," said Jenny. "We only live two doors away.

Josh's dad is a police inspector and Josh's mum is a journalist. She's a reporter on the local newspaper."

"Oh, oh, how interesting. Joshua is lucky to have such interesting parents," said Ms Carter and she started to prowl around her office. She moved piles of paper from one place to another; she brushed the curtains with her hand and pulled off several healthy looking leaves from a tall plant next to the coffee table. After several more questions, Ms Carter sat down behind her desk. "Well thank you, girls," she said looking directly at Suzy and Jenny. "You've been most helpful. You see I wanted to talk to you about Joshua because you were sitting next to him in assembly this morning. I suppose he's in Maths right now. I think I'll have a little chat with him now." Ms Carter leaned forward close to Jenny, "Go and get him for me, Jenny. I'd like to see him."

Jenny looked at Suzy. Suzy's mouth fell open and they both looked back startled at Ms Carter.

"Go on girls, away with you. Go and find me Joshua."

Suzy took a deep breath. "Well Ms Carter, I don't think we can. We haven't seen him since assembly.

"Don't be silly, Suzy. You were sitting either side of him, I saw you."

"But that's it," said Suzy. "He's disappeared."

"What, run away from school?" said Ms Carter in pretend horror.

"No, not run away, Miss. Disappeared," said Jenny. "He just kind of vanished in assembly."

"Jenny, you really must control your imagination. I know you are a creative child but really. You mustn't get carried away. If Joshua is not in your Maths lesson, there must be some other explanation. I'll talk to your teacher. I'm sure there's a logical explanation."

"You could always phone his mum, Miss," said Jenny.

"No, that won't be necessary. I'll get to the bottom of this, leave it to me. Now you two return to your class and, err... you don't need to discuss this with anyone. No one else needs to know about this. Do you understand?"

Suzy and Jenny both nodded silently and Ms Carter waved them out of her office.

"Crikey, what are we going to do?" said Suzy outside in the corridor. "She knows Josh has disappeared but she doesn't know where he is! Poor Josh, he could be anywhere. He could be hurt. She might have killed him. What will his mum say? She's an evil woman," continued Suzy. "She's a witch that's what she is, a witch. We'd better tell the police. I've never liked her-her strict rules, her *scratchy* uniform and her smart clothes."

Jenny was only half listening; she'd heard Suzy rant before. "Smart clothes and flashy jewellery," continued Suzy.

"That's it!" said Jenny, grabbing Suzy's arm. "That's it. It's the flashy jewellery. You saw those colours in assembly; you saw those lights around Josh when she clicked her fingers at him. She set off some powerful force field that made Josh disappear. We'd better tell her; perhaps she can reverse it and get him back."

"But that's stupid," said Suzy. "She'll think we're mad and what if the power is real, she might use it on us."

"Look, we've got to help Josh," said Jenny. "Carter seems pretty desperate and she knows we know what happened, that's why she called us to her office. If she knew how the power worked, she'd have used it on us already. Come on, we must help." Jenny, in her enthusiasm knocked on Ms Carter's door and walked straight in. Ms Carter was slumped forward on her desk with her head in her hands. She looked up startled as Jenny and Suzy walked in. She picked up her two pear drop-shaped earrings which were on the desk.

"You knock and wait" shouted Ms Carter "knock and wait."

As Ms Carter looked up Jenny and Suzy noticed blue mascara running down Ms Carter's cheeks. They saw that her eyes were red and her face was grey and unhappy. Ms Carter reached for a tissue. She wiped her eyes and blew her nose. " Hay fever, a dreadful thing-my eyes, my nose, even my ears ache. I was just trying to put my earrings back in. Sometimes you have to suffer a little to retain standards. You'll find out one day, girls. I suffer very badly at this time of year.

Now what do you want, now that you've barged into my office?"

Jenny took Ms Carter through her theory about the lights; the bracelet, Ms Carter's clicking fingers and the power. Ms Carter listened.

"Oh, I don't know," she said. "It all sounds so incredible. How could I make people disappear? It's impossible. I don't know."

"I'm convinced it was the bracelet," said Jenny. "All those bright lights, I've never seen you wear it in school before. It's beautiful. It may be powerful."

"Well, I have worn it before, young lady," said Ms Carter tersely. "It's my usual accessory for my... this suit. I remember wearing it when Charles Peterson, the poet, came to talk to us.

Suzy knew she was in danger of saying too much about what Ms Carter was wearing so she decided to keep quiet.

"Perhaps you were thinking powerful thoughts about Josh when you clicked your fingers," said Jenny.

"Well, I did want him to stop what he was doing and listen to me. Come to think of it, I may have wished he'd go away if he couldn't behave."

"That's it," said Suzy. "The power comes from a combination of your thoughts, the click and the bracelet. Try clicking again and this time, make nice thoughts about Josh – wish he would come back. Wish hard, Ms Carter."

Ms Carter frowned and looked at Suzy and Jenny. "I don't know," she said. "I don't know, but I do want Joshua back here safe in school. I'll give anything a try."
Ms Carter pointed her arm and thought nice thoughts about Josh. She clicked her fingers – nothing.

"Try it again," said Jenny.

Ms Carter sighed and pointed and clicked three more times. Still no sign of Josh.

"Right, that's enough. This magic stuff – your theory about lights and thoughts is nonsense. I know you mean well, girls, but it's time for a more logical approach. I'm sure Joshua is in school somewhere. You can help me look for him. You know what sorts of things he likes to do. He likes to read a lot, doesn't he? Let's start off in the library." Ms Carter ushered Suzy and Jenny out into the corridor. "I'm sure we'll find him if we look hard," said Ms Carter.

As they strode along the corridor Suzy reflected on what Ms Carter had said. Suzy just knew it was the bracelet. The lights, the sounds were all too powerful. Suzy needed some time to think without Ms Carter bothering her.

"I need to go to the toilet, Miss," she announced. "Can I catch you up in the library?" Suzy hurried into the cloakroom.

She was looking for her bag which was hanging on her peg in the cloakroom. I need to check out the details, she thought to herself. Suzy dived into her bag and pulled out the Carter-watch diary.

Now then, Charles Peterson, the poet, I remember his visit. It was around my birthday. In fact, I think it was 12th March. Suzy opened the Carter-watch diary to the week of 12th March. Let's see, let's see. She quickly read through each day's Carter-watch observations for that week. Monday – no. Tuesday – no. Wednesday – powder blue miniskirt, lemon blouse, gold necklace and YES! Multi coloured bracelet. The entry was in Jenny's writing, she'd even written 'beautiful!' after the bracelet. Well she has worn it before, so what happened this time? Suzy checked the Carter-watch diary again; suit, blouse, bracelet, necklace. Wait a minute, where are the earrings? There's no mention of those hideous pear drop earrings. That's it, that's it! Suzy replaced the Carter-watch diary and hurried out of the cloakroom. On the way she noticed Josh's rucksack hanging on his peg. She knew it was his because it had a computer magazine sticking out of the top. This might come in useful she thought to herself and she took it with her down the corridor. She crept past Ms Carter's office. The door was open and she saw Ms Carter's earrings on her desk. She ran in and picked them up. Ms Carter and Jenny were just coming out of the library. Suzy could tell by their faces that they had not found Josh. Quickly, Suzy threw Josh's rucksack on the floor outside the computer room.

"Ms Carter, Ms Carter," said Suzy "I thought you might need these," and she handed Ms Carter her pear drop earrings. "I know you encourage us to be smart at all times." Ms Carter frowned and took her earrings. Rather

hurriedly she fixed them to her ears. Suzy sensed her chance. "Oh look! Oh look. There's Josh's bag, Miss! He must still be in school." Ms Carter swung round and saw the bag on the floor.

"Yes, that's it," said Ms Carter. "That's Joshua's bag. I've told him before about that computer magazine." Instinctively she stretched out her arm and clicked her fingers at the bag. Suddenly, refracted coloured lights shot around the corridor. A Tibetan wind chime played from Ms Carter's bracelet. Suzy's hair moved in a gentle breeze.

Ms Carter, Suzy and Jenny all stood still waiting for something to happen. Nothing did.

"Pick it up, Jenny, pick it up. Put it on his peg for him. What an untidy boy," Ms Carter said as she opened the door to the computer room. Inside at a computer in the corner, sat a somewhat puzzled looking Josh. He was manipulating a 3D graph on the screen.

"Joshua Atkins, what do you think you are doing in here?" screamed Ms Carter. "You should be in Maths. You don't seem to know where you should be half the time in school. You need to sharpen up. And tidy yourself up. Look at you! Your tie is a mess, your shirt is hanging out of your trousers and Suzy here found your school bag outside in the corridor, not on its peg. When did you last comb your hair?"

"But Miss, you sent me here to..."

"No, I did not. Don't argue with me, young man. Now get back to class. Two Golden Silence class points deducted for your poor organisational skills."

Josh stuffed his shirt into his trousers and straightened his tie. On his way out he snatched his bag from Suzy. "Thanks a lot" he muttered.

When Josh had left, Ms Carter turned to Suzy and Jenny. She was smiling out of the side of her mouth. She looked slightly down her nose and frowned at them. "Now girls," she said and she nodded her head up and down at them so they should agree with what she said. Suzy narrowed her eyes and Jenny

tightened her mouth. "Now girls," said Ms Carter. "Let's have no more silly talk about powers and disappearing. There are more important things for you to be doing than wandering around the school. You've missed a lot of your Maths lesson. Tell Mrs Johnson you were helping me with an important item of lost property. You don't need to go into detail. You don't need to talk to anyone and I mean anyone else about our... misunderstanding this morning. Good, now if that's all clear, straighten yourselves up, look ship shape and return to your class."

Suzy and Jenny turned to leave. "Socks, Jenny, socks," shouted Ms Carter. As they reached the door, Suzy felt her heart beating faster and faster. She felt anger spread over her body but she managed to smile sweetly as she turned to Ms Carter.

"Oh Ms Carter," said Suzy. "There's just one thing. Do you ever read 'Go Girl' magazine?"

Ms Grant's Electric Treatment

Wendy Grant was quietly singing to herself as she ran to school. Not every head teacher runs to their school but Wendy Grant does. Every morning at 6.45, she sets off from her house to jog to Bloxworth School, where she is the head teacher.

Wendy was singing the school song that she had introduced to the school when she became the new head teacher three years ago: "Bloxworth School, Bloxworth School, always work hard and play by the rules. Bloxworth School, Bloxworth School, always work hard and play by the rules." Everyone sang the song every day at the end of assembly. Wendy knew it was one of her innovations.

Wendy continued her running. She passed

the village bakery. The lights were on and loaves were being taken out of ovens. She rounded the corner from the High Street onto the village green. Ah, Wendy loves the village green. It's what makes Bloxworth School special. The school is tucked away in the far corner, surrounded by fields and a few thatched cottages. It was, it is, beautiful, but you have to know it's there. Most visitors to the school get lost when they try to find it for the first time. It's one of those places that's easy to walk to but hard to find by car. The children and their parents like it that way, it's safe, secure and tucked-away.

Wendy ran on across the green. She realised how lucky she was. She has a wonderful job. She lives in a beautiful village with easy access to the motorway. She is popular with the children. The parents like her and the school governors tell her she is doing a good job. Why then did Wendy feel uneasy

as she ran off the village green, along the footpath and into the school?

She stopped at the door and checked her watch. "Sixteen minutes, seventeen seconds. Better than yesterday. Still in line for my improvement target," Wendy said to herself. She started to sing again,

"Bloxworth School, Bloxworth School, always work hard and play by the rules. Bloxworth School, Bloxworth School, always work hard and play by the rules".

Wendy was in school on time and on target. Now she had to make the transformation from early morning jogger to educational leader. She made her way to her newly installed executive shower, her first innovation at Bloxworth School. Governors had agreed that builders should convert a cupboard between her office and the school secretary's into a staff shower room. Mrs Carter, the school secretary

didn't like it at first, but she soon realised that she could stand her umbrella in it on wet mornings, and she could see it made Wendy happy. Mrs Carter likes to keep Wendy happy.

In no time at all, Wendy had showered and changed into her leather trouser suit. She was at her desk and working by 7.30.

At 7.45 Wendy waited for the knock at the door. It came. "Knock knock, tea for the lark. One sugar and two digestives," Colin Patterson said as he came into her office with a tray of tea and biscuits. Colin did this every morning and Wendy was very grateful. Colin, the school caretaker was Wendy's first new staff appointment after she became head teacher. He was very pleased to get the job.

"You spoil me, Colin," said Wendy.

"Well, someone's got to look after you, boss," said Colin. "You work too hard. I'm surprised you have time to eat."

"Don't forget we've got the fire company in this morning checking the alarms, and that Mrs Johnson from the school governors wants me to dig up that paving slab in the school wild area at 10.30 this morning."

Colin raised his eyebrows and shrugged at the mention of Mrs Johnson. Wendy did the same, and then returned to her papers on the desk. She had lots of things to do before the children arrived. She still had to prepare and there was the 8.15 morning staff briefing. She was just about to write the 'important points for today' note when her eye caught the latest education department booklet that was lying on her desk.

"*Pathway to Success*" the booklet was called. 'Make your school a *Pathway to Success*. Don't remain an educational backwater. Plan your pathway through leadership and staff development.'

Instantly, Wendy knew what had been

troubling her as she had jogged across the green earlier. The village, the green, the school, Bloxworth is off the beaten track. Bloxworth is in a backwater. It might be safe and secure but that's not what the Education Department want. They want a *Pathway to Success*. Wendy knew she wanted to lead Bloxworth School along that pathway, so she stopped what she was doing and read the Education Department booklet from cover to cover.

Twenty minutes later, Wendy was standing in the staff room of Bloxworth School. She was looking at her watch and tapping her foot, waiting for Mrs Kendal to arrive. All the other staff were present, it was just Mrs Kendal. She always manages to be four minutes late. Finally, Mrs Kendal flew into the staff room. "Sorry, sorry," she said, "trouble with the photocopier." No one said anything and Mrs Kendal went to sit down. She stopped herself

when she noticed that everyone was standing. There were plenty of empty seats but everyone was standing in a circle around the coffee table.

"Early morning meetings are meant to be crisp and efficient," Wendy announced. "From now on, we will all stand for early morning staff meetings. We'll get the business done quicker if we're all on time, of course," and she threw a withering look at Mrs Kendall. "I want to put Bloxworth School on the Educational Roadmap" she told the teachers. "From now on, we're going to be a striving school. We're going to be running along the pathway to success. From now on, we're on the move."

Time moved at Bloxworth. The teachers strived as they stood through early morning briefings in autumn, winter and into spring. Wendy led the way as she followed the

advice in the booklet *"Pathway to Success."*
As well as early morning briefings, Wendy
introduced two extra evening staff meetings
every week. She wanted to *empower* the
teachers, *encourage them to innovate, set
them free.*

But nothing much changed.

"If anything, the teachers seem to grumble
a bit more now," Wendy said to her local
educational inspector as they talked about
the progress of Bloxworth School.

"Oh, they're all good teachers," said
Wendy. "They work hard, but it's all so safe
and all so secure. I want them to be
innovators but the only new ideas they seem
to come up with are ideas for new furniture
for the staff room. They say it's overcrowded,
they say it's not comfortable. They say they
didn't want a shower, they wanted a
dishwasher. I suppose the staffroom could do
with a tidy up. I've noticed a few buttons are

coming off the chair covers. But honestly! I want them to give me new teaching ideas, new ways towards success and all they do is grumble. Do you know, I think the teachers have a problem. I think they're too content."

Content was not a word used by the teachers in the staff room. They were fed up with the mess, fed up with the piles of paper and fed up with all the extra meetings. They all secretly agreed that the best thing to do was to keep quiet when Wendy was talking and just nod in agreement at things she said.

"Let her find the pathway, we'll all follow," said Mrs Simpson, the Class 6 teacher.

"My back is playing up from these chairs," said Mrs Richards from Class 2.

"That new shower could have paid for a whole new suite of furniture."

"And I've ruined three good sweaters on these chair buttons," said Mrs Sak from class 1. "Pathway to success...I'd rather find a pathway to the door."

So, things were not going well for Wendy. Her running times to school were getting slower. Colin had noticed this, and one morning he opened Wendy's office door with the usual cup of tea and two biscuits, and she wasn't there, just an empty chair and a cluttered desk. No smiling Wendy. Colin was just leaving the office when he heard a car pull into the school car park. Wendy got out. She looked tired, she looked unhappy. Colin knew something was wrong, Wendy had driven to school.

Somehow Colin and Wendy ended up talking for a long time. They started with tea, went onto native Yorkshire, and finally, Wendy's troubles. Colin listened well and Wendy found herself explaining about "Pathway to Success" and the staff room furniture and teachers who were 'content'. Colin put down his teacup and stood up.

Wendy felt embarrassed and shuffled some papers on her desk. She looked at Colin. Colin looked into her watery eyes. "Don't worry, boss," he said, "I can help. I know what you need. You need one of those 'spark your body into life' stimulators. I've seen them on cable TV and I think you can get them on the Internet. 'Electrospark', I think they're called.

"Electrospark," said Wendy. "Spark is certainly what's needed. What does it do? What is it?"

"It's a sort of pad that works on your muscles. I think it gives a small electrostatic shock and it vibrates. It's meant to help stimulate you into action and give you energy. Shall I order you one? You could give it a try. If it's any good you could get one for the staffroom. The teachers are always saying they want new staffroom equipment."

Wendy looked at Colin. She looked at his

calm, smiling eyes and his helpful expression. "Yes please," she said. "Let's give it a go."

It took ten days for the Electrospark to arrive. Colin stayed late with Wendy in her office to try it out.

"It's quite simple, boss," said Colin. "You just stick this little round pad on your arm and then you press the remote control and you should feel stimulated and ready for action."

Colin rolled up his shirt sleeve, stuck the pad on his upper arm and then said, "Ready, boss, give it a go."

Wendy pressed the remote control. Colin jumped a little and smiled. He stood up and ran on the spot.

"Ooh, it's great," he said. "It tingles a bit but it really gets you going. I feel like I could run a marathon."

"Do you think it will work on teachers?" Wendy asked.

"I'm sure it will," said Colin. "Give it a go,

boss."

Wendy took the pad and stuck it on her arm. Colin pressed the button.

"Wow," said Wendy. "This is the ticket. This is what I...my staff need."

Wendy and Colin tried the Electrospark several times. They stuck it on their arms, ankles and hands. It worked every time. Colin and Wendy found themselves laughing and dancing around Wendy's office.

"This is great, Colin," said Wendy. "This will stimulate the staff. This will put Bloxworth on the *Pathway to Success*. Thank you so much, Colin. You've helped me solve a big problem." Wendy held Colin's hand and looked into his eyes.

"That's ok, boss," said Colin and his face went bright red as he pulled away from Wendy's gaze.

"Colin, please call me Wendy," said Wendy.

The next school staff meeting was two

days away. Colin agreed to help Wendy with her Electrospark plan to stimulate the teachers. They decided that Colin would hide the Electrospark pad in one of the broken buttons on a chair in the staffroom. When a teacher sat against the button, on the Electrospark chair, all Wendy had to do was press the remote control and 'spark' the teacher into action. The remote control was small and Wendy disguised it by putting it on a key ring, so that it looked like a car key.

Wendy arrived first and made sure she sat opposite the Electrospark chair, or the 'action chair' as she came to call it. Gradually the teachers filed into their second staff meeting of the week. Wendy was delighted to see that it was Mrs Kendal who sat in the 'action chair'.

For twenty minutes the staff meeting took its usual course. Wendy talking, the teachers nodding. Soon it got to the bit where Wendy asked for suggestions and new ideas. Silence.

Mrs Kendal, who had been sitting forward in her chair, leant back.

"Got you," thought Wendy, as Mrs Kendal's back hit the back of the chair. Wendy pressed the remote control. There was a short pause before Mrs Kendal smiled, rose to her feet, and announced to everyone that she was "going to do something."

"I've been listening to what you said, Wendy," said Mrs Kendal. "It sounds fascinating. I volunteer to lead a sustained literacy drive with years 1, 2 and 3. I'll start with a phonetic learning resource bank and develop it into a writing strategy for the older pupils."

Everyone was stunned. The teachers looked at each other. They looked at Wendy. Mrs Kendal looked red, nervous and a little surprised.

Wendy smiled at Mrs Kendal, "Splendid, Sarah," she said. "Thank you very much."

86

Over the next few weeks and months, Wendy used the action chair a lot. By carefully making sure that each teacher sat in the chair, Wendy ensured that Bloxworth had six new initiatives in place. A literary development strategy, a problem solving approach to maths, learning history through drawing, computers for learning not for fun, integrated cross-curricular dance studies and music makes you smarter. Wendy had put Bloxworth School clearly on the road to success. Bloxworth was visited by lots of advisors and teachers from other schools. Bloxworth School was in the newspapers. It was designated a **Pathway Leader School** by the Department of Education. Bloxworth was on the map.

If only Wendy had left it there. After a year of innovation and development, grumbling started amongst the parents and governors. "There are too many visitors to

the school," they said. "The village green is being spoiled by all the cars. The school is too full." There weren't enough places for all of the children whose parents wanted to send their children to the school. A special governors' meeting was called to sort out the difficulties. Wendy was a bit put out that all her innovation wasn't being appreciated. As she sat in the staffroom with the governors, she noticed that the Chairman of Governors was sitting in the action chair. "He needs a bit more spark, he needs to get with us on the path," thought Wendy, and she decided to use the Electrospark on the Chairman of Governors. He finished talking about staff workload and stress and sat back in the chair. Wendy pressed the remote control. Nothing happened. She pressed it again and again. She didn't stop until another governor, Mrs Johnson, said, 'Can anyone else smell burning?"

"I can that," said Councillor Adams, "I think our Chairman of Governors is on fire." Smoke was pouring from the back of the action chair. The Chairman of Governors leapt to his feet. Flames were coming from the back of his jacket. Councillor Adams shouted "Fire! Fire!" The Chairman of Governors danced

around the room trying to take off his jacket.

"Help! Help!" cried Mrs Johnson. Mr Reece, a parent governor grabbed a fire extinguisher. He sprayed the Chairman of Governors from head to foot with white foam. He did the same to the action chair and quickly the fire was put out. A frozen silence fell on the special governors, Meeting. Wendy hid the Electrospark remote control in her handbag. The Chairman of Governors wiped foam away from his eyes. He stood shaking and angry in the middle of the room. He kicked the action chair before regaining control of himself. Then, very loudly, he shouted. "This staffroom is a tip. It's not safe. It needs to be re-furbished. I propose we vote money for an immediate refurbishment. Get rid of this old furniture. Let's make it comfortable for the teachers."

"Hear, hear," said everyone. The motion was passed.

If you visit Bloxworth School now, it's still hard to find. You can still hear birds sing, you can still enjoy beautiful views. But you won't find a scruffy staffroom. There are no action chairs. There is a new teacher's conservatory and lounge. It's plush, luxurious and comfortable. It has its own pathway.

Bloxworth School now has a new headteacher and a new caretaker. Wendy has moved on to another job; she is a New Labour MP in London. Colin is in charge of a smart new apartment block on the River Thames. He and Wendy live together in the studio flat on the top floor. They have a new baby daughter. They've called her Electra. Bloxworth is safe and secure.

Everyone is content.

Until the next time.

Bob Beesley Remembered

Mrs Williams was having trouble with the kettle in the staffroom. She complained to her friend and colleague, Jean Wilkins. "It's no good, Jean, if I can't start my day with a cuppa. I'm at sixes and sevens all morning. Surely the school can afford a new kettle. Never mind, I'll nip down to the infant's department. They've got their own kettle down there. I'll use theirs. Be a love, put a note on that one for Bob. I'm sure he'll fix it when he comes in."

Bob Beesley does fix things, that's what he's known for in Moorgrove Primary School. Bob Beesley teaches year six and he fixes things. He's done this for twenty seven years. Moorgrove was his first teaching job and it's going to be his last, because Bob Beesley is

taking early retirement at the end of the term. He and Mrs Beesley are going to travel Europe in their camper van, "Before it's too late", Bob says.

Edward Robert Beesley joined the teaching staff of Moorgrove Primary School in 1976. He trained as a science teacher and he likes finding out how things work. That's why he likes fixing things. He talks like a scientist; "What you need to do..." "If you consider the technical options..." "Let's look at it logically" are a few of his favourite phrases. He fixes things for children and he mends things for the school. He wears a jumper with a tie in winter and sandals when it's hot in summer. He drives the school minibus, manages the football team and never shouts at anyone. Everyone agrees Bob Beesley is OK.

When Bob arrived at Moorgrove in 1976, he liked it so he stayed. He liked the then

headteacher, Mrs Hudson. He liked his light and airy classroom and most of all he liked his spacious toilet.

You see, for most of his long career, Bob has been surrounded by women at work. This has had its disadvantages – he has to talk about football with Year Six and he hates healthy salad "working lunches" but it's also had its upside; Bob has his own exclusive toilet. The male staff toilet over the years has become Bob's place. He's developed it as the school has grown. When the first new building work was done, Bob asked for cupboards to be put in and he fixed his own extra shelves. Since then, he's brought boxes from home and filled them with useful things. Bob's toilet is a cave of hidden treasures, full of useful tools, spare bits and pieces and 'that'll come in handy' throw aways that he has collected. Bob's toilet is where the kettle will be mended, it's where what you need is

found. It's also where Bob goes to get away. Since the building of the new visitors' toilets, he's hardly disturbed at all. Most of the women teachers make jokes about Bob and his toilet. "How's the weather in there, Bob?" they jibe, or "Have you got a bed for it yet?" "Do you let it out for meetings?" but Bob doesn't mind. If he needs to fix something at playtime, he can pop in and do it without being disturbed. He's spent many a lunchtime "getting on" in his toilet. If he's not in the staffroom, the other teachers know where he is. If he's needed, they send a child from Year Six to go and get him. Everyone knows to go straight to Bob's toilet and knock on the door.

Today it was William Saunders' turn to go and find Mr Beesley. Mrs Wilkins sent for him at 9.05. She has the class next door and when she heard too much noise, she popped in and saw that Bob wasn't there.

"Go and tell Mr Beesley school has started, will you, William?" she said and William Saunders automatically strode off to Bob's toilet. He knocked and waited. "Mr Beesley, Mrs Wilkins says it's time for school. Lessons are starting. We're all waiting."

"Mr Beesley" (silence).

"Mr Beesley, are you in there?"

William Saunders wanted to get on with things. He knocked on the door again and opened it gingerly. He popped his head round the door. Inside he saw the cupboards, the boxes, the workbench, the electrical gadgets, the tins of household paint, the coffee maker, the collection of railway magazines, the garden chair, the bicycle frame and hundreds of other things. But he could not see Mr Beesley. He went back and reported to Mrs Wilkins. "Well, you'd better let Mrs Gordon know," said Mrs Wilkins. "Perhaps he's been held up. I'll take the register, tell

Mrs Gordon she's needed in your class."

Mrs Gordon, the headteacher of Moorgrove School, was surprised when William told her that Mr Beesley wasn't in school. She gave a puzzled look to Mrs Carlton, the school secretary. "Not like Bob," said Mrs Carlton. "He's hardly ever off ill, usually drags himself in even if he's poorly."

"Well, I'll go and cover his class. Perhaps you could finish these figures on your own and give Bob's home number a ring to find out where he is."

Mrs Gordon followed William back to his class. "Thursday morning ,William," she said. "What do you have timetabled in this morning? It's maths, isn't it? We'll start with ...no, no wait a minute," she said to herself before turning to William again. "Never mind, William, I've got an idea of my own. We'll do something special this morning." she said with a smile.

Inside the classroom, Mrs Gordon made an announcement. "Well, as you can see class 6b, we don't have Mr Beesley yet. He's probably stuck in traffic. You'll have to put up with me for a while. So I thought I'd make use of the fact that Mr Beesley is not here. You all know that Mr Beesley is retiring at the end of the term after long and special service to the school. Obviously we're all going to miss him, so it would be really good if we could give him something special to remind him of his time here in the school. He's been here a long time, you know. He's taught quite a number of your mums and dads as well as you."

"He taught my mum, Miss"

"Yes I know, Jason."

"And mine."

"That's right, he did, Samantha."

"And my dad, Miss."

"Yes, yes, I know. Look, all of you have come to know Mr Beesley well and some of

you know about him through what your parents have told you. While he's not here this morning, can we collect some of our special memories about Mr Beesley? Perhaps you remember some special things you did with him in school or some funny incident in class or a story your mum and dad have told you about him. I'd like you all to sit quietly and think about him for a while, then perhaps we can share a few memories together. Later we can write them all down and make a book to give to Mr Beesley as a leaving present. I'm sure he will enjoy it. He can take it with him on his tour of Europe. Let's keep this a secret though. We want it to be a surprise. If Mr Beesley suddenly appears, we'll pretend we're doing mental maths. I'll suddenly throw a Maths question at someone, that will disguise what we're doing. Be ready to pretend if Mr Beesley arrives.

Right then. We'll give ourselves until 9.30 to

sit and think quietly about our memories of Mr Beesley."

An unusual stillness descended on Class 6b, broken only by sniffing from Wendy Burton. "Do you need a tissue, Wendy?" asked Mrs Gordon.

"No, Miss, it's just...I feel a bit weird...I don't like thinking back about Mr Beesley when he's not here. It's a bit scary. I'm scared, Mrs Gordon. Can I read my book for a minute? Can I not think about Mr Beesley, just for a minute? It's just now, Mrs Gordon I'm really scared. It's just now. I only need a couple of minutes. I'll think about Mr Beesley then.

"Goodness me, Wendy, you're a strange one. Take a couple of minutes if you have to. Compose yourself, then you can join in with the rest of us later."

Wendy gave Mrs Gordon a watery smile and opened her reading book. At 9.17 the room returned to silence. You could hear

brains thinking. Happy memories filled the
air. Every so often a smile broke out on a
face or an eyebrow was raised as memory
pictures flashed inside the heads of class 6b.
Mrs Gordon joined in too. She found herself
smiling as she remembered a particular staff
meeting when Bob showed off his newest
invention, a gas propelled toy car that
"demonstrated" the fundamental principles
of pressure, force and movement. It shot
straight across the staffroom floor into Jean
Wilkins' handbag. Tissues went everywhere.
Mrs Gordon's own memories of Bob Beesley
were so strong she'd forgotten the time and
it was 9.50 before she called the class
together again to share memories and
stories. "Goodness me, look at the time," she
said. "Right class 6b, we've got a lot to
share and not much time. Alan, you keep a
special eye on the door. If you see Mr
Beesley coming, shout out "42, Miss," and

that will be the signal for us all to stop talking about Mr Beesley. We'll then pretend we're doing mental maths. Right then, who wants to start? Who's got a really good story about Mr Beesley?"

Hands shot up around the classroom. "Alright, well done, what a lot. I'm not sure we'll have time for everyone. Let's start with you Ross."

"Mine's about the time he took us to football against St. Alfred's, Miss."

"I think I know what's coming, Ross. Do we really have to?"

"Oh, it's really funny, Miss. I know Mr Beesley is really nice but against St. Alfred's he really lost it. You know when you get into the school football team, he keeps going on and on about what an honour it is and how you represent the team and that winning is not important and ..."

"Well, he's quite right" interrupted Mrs

Gordon.

"Yeah, yeah, I know we all know but this time Miss, this time against St. Alfred's, he gave us the usual talk in the minibus on the way then when we were playing he really lost it. We've played St. Alfred's before and they're really dirty. Anyway, we were winning 2-1 with 10 minutes left, when their teacher sent on their substitutes. They were really good and really big. I looked around and I could see Mr Beesley shouting at the referee, something about the players being too old and not registered. Anyway, these three subs played really well and scored twice. Mr Beesley was running up and down the side of the pitch screaming and shouting and arguing with the other teacher. We played on but we lost 2-3. After the match Mr Beesley told us to get straight on to the minibus, that we'd get changed back at school. When we got on the bus I saw Mr

Beesley pick up the trainer's water bucket and...and he emptied it into the St. Alfred's teacher's sports bag. Then he hurried back and started to drive us away. When the other teacher picked up his bag, water went everywhere; all over his shoes, all over the spare kit. He was furious. He waved his fist at Mr Beesley as we drove off. We were all killing ourselves laughing – but no one dared say anything to Mr Beesley."

"Uhm, yes, thank you Ross. I did hear about that little incident and you do know that St. Alfred's was expelled from the school league for playing over age players. Let's say that story is an example of Mr Beesley's sense of fair play. Rachel, you had your hand up. What's your story?"

"Well, Miss. This is a story from my mum really. You know Mr Beesley taught my mum. Well, this was back in the old days when teachers went on strike or something. Mum

says it was to do with money. Anyway my mum was at school, but for a while, all the teachers refused to look after the kids at lunch time and they all went out at lunch time and so all the kids had to go home. My mum went to my Gran's for dinner past Cox's lay-by – you know Cox's lay-by up past Woodford Road on the Lower Road?"

"Yes, yes, Rachel."

"Well, my mum got near the lay-by and she saw Mr Beesley's camper van, a really old fashioned orange one and Mr Beesley and all the teachers were sitting outside his van in little deck chairs having a picnic. Mr Beesley had a little gas stove and he was boiling a kettle and mum said she could hear all the teachers laughing and talking like they were on holiday. Well, mum went to my Gran's for dinner and on her way back to school in the afternoon, she saw Mr Beesley's camper van still in Cox's lay-by but no-one

was around, all the teachers had gone but mum said she thought she heard some one shouting 'help, help!' but she couldn't see anyone, so she carried on back to school. When she got to school none of the teachers were there and Mrs Jewel, the old headteacher had to take the whole school in the hall for singing practice. My mum says that half way through "Give me joy in my heart" everyone stopped singing as they looked out of the window and saw Mr Beesley's orange camper van slowly coming into the school playground. One of the old teachers was steering and all the other teachers were pushing. Mr Beesley was shouting instructions. My mum said it was really, really so funny that everyone burst out laughing, even Mrs Jewel smiled. You see, Mr Beesley and all the teachers had had a picnic, got back in the camper van to come back to school but something was wrong

with Mr Beesley's van. They all got locked in and Mr Beesley had to break a window to let everyone out and they all had to push the van back to school. My mum still goes on about it, Miss."

"Yes, I'm sure she does, Rachel. Thank you. Thank you. So far girls and boys we've had two funny stories about Mr Beesley. Does anyone have anything – shall we say, a little more – substantial? You have, have you, William?"

"Yes Miss. This is about my dad. My dad was in Mr Beesley's class and he's always going on about the things Mr Beesley taught him. He says if it wasn't for Mr Beesley, he would never have become a scientist. My dad's a physicist at the University, Miss."

"Yes I know William."

"Well, my dad says it was Mr Beesley's experiments in school that made him interested in science . He says Mr Beesley let them make up their own experiments every

week. Mr Beesley used to make everyone design their own machines and test them, and everyone in my dad's class had to get the things they needed to make their machines. Mr Beesley always helped if they couldn't get them. Anyway, my dad made loads of machines and nearly all of them worked properly but, this is the important bit, my dad says Mr Beesley made him solve problems using scientific principles. He always says what a good science teacher Mr Beesley is. My dad's still got some of the things he made with Mr Beesley. Why can't we do that every week, Miss? Why can't we build things ourselves, Miss?"

"You still can, William. I'm sure Mr Beesley won't let you forget science, William. We just have a lot more to do in schools these days, which, goodness me! Look at the time. It's nearly playtime. I'm sorry, we'll have to finish sharing our thoughts about Mr Beesley another

time." Class 6b moaned. "I know, I'm sorry, I was enjoying it too" said Mrs Gordon." Look, later on this week I'll arrange a time when I take you again. I'll send Mr Beesley on a little job and while he's away, we can all write these happy memories down and stick them in a book to give to Mr Beesley on the last day of term. Mind you, he didn't arrive out of the blue so we've kept our secret from him.

Right, one minute before bell time. A challenge for those of you who were left waiting to share your story about Mr Beesley, condense your story into one sentence and we'll go round the room. You start Samantha."

"Mr Beesley and the hot air balloon."

"Mr Beesley and his big shorts."

"Mr Beesley locks Jason in the cupboard."

"Mr Beesley mends my violin."

"Mr Beesley's maths tests."

"Mr Beesley and the mouse that escaped."

Each memory was greeted with "oh yes"

or "I remember that" from other people in the class. Finally it was Harry Richards turn.

"Sugar lumps", he said, and the whole class burst out laughing.

"Ah yes!" said Mrs Gordon ,"few of us here will ever forget the sugar lumps experiment! We must make sure that goes in the book. Come on now, off you go, out to play and remember, not a word to Mr Beesley."

As the children left for morning play, Wendy Burton sidled up to Mrs Gordon.

"I still don't like it without Mr Beesley," she said. "Please Miss, can I go and see if he's here yet? Perhaps he's just late and he's in his cupboard. Can I go and see, Miss. Please, Miss."

"Very well, Wendy" said Mrs Gordon. "If you have to, you go and check Mr Beesley's toilet and I'll go and speak to Mrs Carlton. Perhaps she knows where he is. Come and let me know if you find him,Wendy."

Mrs Gordon strode purposefully to the staffroom as Wendy made her way down the school corridor to Mr Beesley's toilet.

"Any news about Bob?" enquired Mrs Gordon, as she helped herself to coffee in the staffroom.

"No. I've tried his home number several times. I just get the answer machine. That's most unusual. Cynthia doesn't work on Thursdays, she's usually at home."

"Well, we'll give him to lunch time, but I can't cover his class this afternoon, I've got a head's meeting. If we've not heard by 11.30, you'll have to get a supply in."

As Mrs Gordon and Mrs Carlton discussed arrangements for a supply teacher for Mr Beesley Wendy Burton knocked on the door of Mr Beesley's toilet. There was no answer. Wendy knocked again but without waiting, she did something that she'd never done before, something that she knew she

shouldn't, but something that today she knew she had to. She quietly opened the door to Mr Beesley's toilet and crept inside.

Back in the staffroom, morning coffee break was in full swing. Teachers were exchanging pieces of paper, biscuits were being passed around. Mrs Carlton interrupted her story about last night's yoga to answer the telephone.

"Oh Cynthia, it's you. I've been trying to get you all morning. We were wondering about...Oh right. Oh fine, yes. I'll put her on,. Mrs Carlton passed the phone to Mrs Gordon. "It's Cynthia, Anne, she says she wants to talk to you urgently. She sounds upset." The staffroom fell silent. Mrs Wilkins held her biscuit halfway to her mouth. Miss Alderman nervously twiddled her hair.

"Yes, hello Cynthia, Anne here. How are you? How's... Oh no, Cynthia, oh no, oh dear God, Oh Cynthia, I am so sorry. Heart attack

you say, this morning 9.30 on his way to school. Cynthia, I'm so sorry. What can I do? Are you on your own?"

Wendy Burton was on her own, inside Mr Beesley's toilet. She was where she shouldn't be but she didn't feel frightened or lonely. After creeping into Mr Beesley's toilet she stood still and took in all that was there. She roamed her eyes around the gadgets, the bike frame, the piles of magazines and the football kit. She noticed the handmade shelves, the labels on things and the smell of Mr Beesley's after shave. A shaft of sunlight gleamed through the frosted glass window and shone onto a bronze coloured key, sticking out of one of the cupboards. Wendy knew she had to open it.

Inside the cupboard Wendy found an old book, a label on the front said "Children's Poems" and Wendy flitted through the collection of handwritten poems that Mr

Beesley had stuck in the book. They all had dates on them. The first one was September 16th 1976. Wendy put it back and picked up the only other thing inside the cupboard, a glass frame covered with a bright yellow duster. As she took off the duster, Wendy stared at the writing on the certificate inside the gleaming frame;

Edward Robert Beesley
Department for Education and Science
1973
Qualified Teacher Number 73/88V471

Wendy held the frame in both hands. The sun outside reflected back from the shiny glass. Wendy smiled. Through every part of her body she felt one hundred different sensations. She heard happy laughter and the music of children singing. She smelt the vegetables on display at school harvest

119

festival. She heard the silence of quiet reading, the cheers at school sports days, the blowing of playtime whistles and the clatter of plastic dinner plates. She smelt the chlorine of the swimming pool mixed with the smell of new books and Mr Beesley's aftershave.

Wendy trembled as her arms held onto a familiar feeling. She felt the warmth of Bob Beesley's hand as her own small, cold hand held on to his in the playground when she was young and just a little frightened. The warmth of the sun in Bob Beesley's toilet spoke to her. It repeated some familiar words, she heard Bob Beesley say;

"You're great, Wendy. You can do it. You've done really well."

Rest in peace Bob Beesley.

Adrian Townsend

Lives in Oxford. He likes playing golf, football

and dominoes as well as writing stories.

He supports Oxford United.

He can be contacted on E mail at

Hidip@aol.com

If you enjoyed this book

Look out for other stories by the same author

Gran's Gang

Gran's Gang Go To Spain

Gran's Gang Solve a Mystery

Powerful Eyes

Naughty Lessons

Thanks to
J Brightmore and Jody Elphick
for layout, book design and image
retouching.

Cover design by
Gavin Anderson
ganderson78@mac.com